BRINGING BACK THE

Snow Leopard

Rachel Stuckey

Crabtree Publishing Company

www.crabtreebooks.com

CRABTREE
PUBLISHING COMPANY
WWW.CRABTREEBOOKS.COM

Author: Rachel Stuckey

Series Research and Development: Reagan Miller

Picture Manager: Sophie Mortimer

Design Manager: Keith Davis

Editorial Director: Lindsey Lowe

Children's Publisher: Anne O'Daly

Editor: Ellen Rodger

Proofreader: Wendy Scavuzzo

Cover design: Margaret Amy Salter

**Production coordinator and
    Prepress technician:** Margaret Amy Salter

Print coordinator: Katherine Berti

Produced for Crabtree Publishing Company
by Brown Bear Books

Photographs
(t=top, b= bottom, l=left, r=right, c=center)

Front Cover: All images from Shutterstock

Interior: Dreamstime: Walter Arce 10, Michael Fitzsimmonds 6, outast85 11b, A B Zerit 15; iStock: FatCamera 29, Guenter Guni 17t, Olivier Le Moal 28, outcast85 9, sdigital 16, Vladislav Strekopytov 5b, Koon Yongyt 17b, A B Zerit 7; Mogabay Wildlife Conservation Society: D. Demelio 12; Nature Picture Library: Oriol Alamany 18, Sebastian Kennerknecht 25, Cyril Ruoso 8, 22; Shutterstock: Artush 21t, De Visu 19t, Aleksandr Denisyuk 4, Dennis W Donohue 1, milosk50 26, Vladimir Mucibabic 27t, Nagel Photography 5t, Sergei Primakov 21b, Andreas Rose 20, tacud 27b, Yury Taranik 11t; Snow Leopard Conservancy: 14. 19b. 24; Snow Leopard Trust: 13.

Brown Bear Books has made every attempt to contact the copyright holder. If you have any information please contact licensing@brownbearbooks.co.uk

Library and Archives Canada Cataloguing in Publication

Title: Bringing back the snow leopard / Rachel Stuckey.
Names: Stuckey, Rachel, author.
Series: Animals back from the brink.
Description: Series statement: Animals back from the brink | Includes index.
Identifiers: Canadiana (print) 20190128267 | Canadiana (ebook) 20190128275 | ISBN 9780778763239 (hardcover) | ISBN 9780778763277 (softcover) | ISBN 9781427123350 (HTML)
Subjects: LCSH: Snow leopard—Juvenile literature. | LCSH: Snow leopard—Conservation—Juvenile literature. | LCSH: Endangered species—Juvenile literature. | LCSH: Wildlife recovery—Juvenile literature.
Classification: LCC QL737.C23 S78 2019 | DDC j333.95/9755516—dc23

Library of Congress Cataloging-in-Publication Data

Names: Stuckey, Rachel, author.
Title: Bringing back the snow leopard / Rachel Stuckey.
Description: New York : Crabtree Publishing Company, [2020] | Series: Animals back from the brink | Includes index.
Identifiers: LCCN 2019025164 (print) | LCCN 2019025165 (ebook) | ISBN 9780778763239 (hardcover) | ISBN 9780778763277 (paperback) | ISBN 9781427123350 (ebook)
Subjects: LCSH: Snow leopard--Conservation--Juvenile literature.
Classification: LCC QL737.C23 S84 2020 (print) | LCC QL737.C23 (ebook) | DDC 599.75/55--dc23
LC record available at https://lccn.loc.gov/2019025164
LC ebook record available at https://lccn.loc.gov/2019025165

Crabtree Publishing Company
www.crabtreebooks.com   1-800-387-7650

Printed in the U.S.A./082019/CG20190712

Published in Canada
Crabtree Publishing
616 Welland Ave.
St. Catharines, Ontario
L2M 5V6

Published in the United States
Crabtree Publishing
PMB 59051
350 Fifth Avenue, 59th Floor
New York, New York 10118

Published in the United Kingdom
Crabtree Publishing
Maritime House
Basin Road North, Hove
BN41 1WR

Published in Australia
Crabtree Publishing
Unit 3–5 Currumbin Court
Capalaba
QLD 4157

Contents

Find videos and extra material online at **crabtreeplus.com** to learn more about the conservation of animals and ecosystems. See page 30 in this book for the access code to this material.

Ghosts of the Mountain

Very few people have ever seen a snow leopard in the wild. Most of these big cats live in the high mountains of Central and South Asia, on the **Tibetan Plateau** and the mountain ranges that surround it. Snow leopards are known as the "ghosts of the mountain" because of the color of their fur, and because they are elusive, or hard to find.

Snow leopards are well adapted to their cold, dry mountain **habitat**. Their coloring gives them **camouflage** in the steep cliffs and rocky **outcrops** of snowy mountains. Their fur is very thick and their paws, which are also covered with thick fur, work like snowshoes. These big cats have short but strong legs, and can jump distances of up to 50 feet (15 m) to catch their **prey**. They can even hunt prey that is three times their weight. Snow leopards hunt wild sheep and goats, but also eat small animals such as hares and birds.

The snow leopard wasn't even photographed until the 1970s, when Dr. George Schaller and his team spotted a female snow leopard sitting on a rocky slope high in the Hindu Kush mountains of northern Pakistan.

SNOW LEOPARD NUMBERS

It has always been hard to estimate the size of the snow leopard population because they live across such a huge geographic **range**. They are also very shy! Currently, experts believe there may be 3,000 to 7,000 snow leopards living in the wild. There are about 600 living in captivity across the globe. As a **predator** at the top of the food chain, snow leopards play an important role in the **ecosystem**. A healthy population of snow leopards helps to keep the entire ecosystem in balance.

Since 2017, scientists have placed up to 150 hidden cameras in the Altai Mountains of Russia. They hope to monitor the numbers of snow leopards living in or passing through the area.

Species at Risk

Created in 1984, the International Union for the **Conservation** of Nature (IUCN) protects wildlife, plants, and **natural resources** around the world. Its members include about 1,400 governments and nongovernmental organizations. The IUCN publishes the Red List of Threatened **Species** each year, which tells people how likely a plant or animal species is to become **extinct**. It began publishing the list in 1964.

The Guam Kingfisher was once found in a wide variety of habitats on the islands of Guam. In 2016 the Red List classified it as Extinct in the Wild (EW). The IUCN updates the Red List twice a year to track the changing of species. Each individual species is reevaluated at least every five years.

SCIENTIFIC CRITERIA

The Red List, created by scientists, divides nearly 80,000 species of plants and animals into nine categories. Criteria for each category include the growth and decline, or falling numbers, of the population size of a species. They also include how many individuals within a species can breed, or have babies. In addition, scientists include information about the habitat of the species, such as its size and quality. These criteria allow scientists to figure out the probability of extinction facing the species.

IUCN LEVELS OF THREAT

The Red List uses nine categories to define the threat to a species.

Extinct (EX)	No living individuals survive
Extinct in the Wild (EW)	Species cannot be found in its natural habitat
Exists only in **captivity**, in **cultivation**, or in an area that is not its natural habitat
Critically Endangered (CR)	At extremely high risk of becoming extinct in the wild
Endangered (EN)	At very high risk of extinction in the wild
Vulnerable (VU)	At high risk of extinction in the wild
Near Threatened (NT)	Likely to become threatened in the near future
Least Concern (LC)	Widespread, abundant, or at low risk
Data Deficient (DD)	Not enough data to make a judgment about the species
Not Evaluated (NE)	Not yet evaluated against the criteria

In the United States, the Endangered Species Act of 1973 was passed to protect species from possible extinction. It has its own criteria for classifying species, but they are similar to those of the IUCN. Canada introduced the Species at Risk Act in 2002. More than 530 species are protected under the act. The list of species is compiled by the Committee on the Status of Endangered Wildlife in Canada (COSEWIC).

SNOW LEOPARD RISK LEVEL

Since 2016, the IUCN Red List has classified the snow leopard as Vulnerable, with a decreasing population of about 3,000 adults. This number is only an estimate. Some studies have provided estimates as high as 7,000, including cubs and young adults. Before 2016, snow leopards were listed as Endangered. Since then, research and conservation methods have improved. However, the gray ghosts of the mountain remain at high risk of extinction.

The Human Threat

Snow leopards face two main threats to their survival: people and climate change. Throughout history, snow leopards have been hunted for their beautiful fur. People sharing the same habitat used snow leopard fur to keep warm. However, in the 1900s, snow leopard furs became a popular worldwide fashion. In the 1920s, around 1,000 **pelts** were traded for sale each year.

Today, it is illegal to hunt the snow leopard, but they are still killed for their body parts, which are used in some traditional medicines in Asia. Illegal hunting is sometimes called poaching. The Convention on International Trade in Endangered Species (CITES) makes selling snow leopard body parts illegal, but poachers make a lot of money. They think it is worth the risk.

This snow leopard pelt was seized by the government anti-poaching team in Kyrgyzstan. Experts believe at least one snow leopard per day is killed illegally.

THE HERDER CONFLICT

Illegal hunting of other species, such as the Siberian ibex, reduces the food supply for snow leopards. Humans moving into the habitat also made it more difficult for the leopard and its prey to survive, so snow leopards began to kill domesticated animals. Herds of sheep and goats made an easy target for the big cat. People who live in the high mountains rely on their sheep and goats for survival. Families have little money, so losing even one animal can be a disaster. The snow leopard is a real threat. Conservationists believe that half the snow leopards illegally killed by humans are killed by herders protecting their animals.

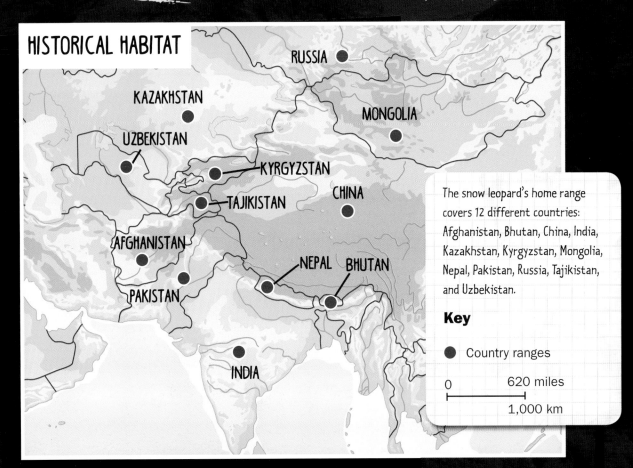

HISTORICAL HABITAT

RUSSIA

KAZAKHSTAN

MONGOLIA

UZBEKISTAN

KYRGYZSTAN

CHINA

TAJIKISTAN

AFGHANISTAN

NEPAL   BHUTAN

PAKISTAN

INDIA

The snow leopard's home range covers 12 different countries: Afghanistan, Bhutan, China, India, Kazakhstan, Kyrgyzstan, Mongolia, Nepal, Pakistan, Russia, Tajikistan, and Uzbekistan.

Key

● Country ranges

0   620 miles

1,000 km

Shrinking Habitat

When many plants and animals in an ecosystem depend on a single species for survival, the species is called a **keystone species**. If it is removed or lost from an ecosystem, the ecosystem changes completely. The snow leopard is a predator keystone species at the top of the food chain. Without these **apex predators**, the delicate balance of the ecosystem begins to change. Other animals start to overpopulate the habitat and change the survival of other species. If the snow leopard survives and thrives, scientists know that the mountain ecosystem is healthy for all plants and animals.

On the Tibetan Plateau, the average temperature has increased by 3° Fahrenheit (1.7°C) in the last 20 years. This may not sound too bad, but such a change can reduce the leopard's habitat by one-third.

HABITAT AND CLIMATE CHANGE

Like all species, snow leopards face a threat from climate change. Snow leopards generally live on the boundary between the snowline and the treeline of mountain ranges. The snowline is the **elevation** above which snow remains on the ground all year. The treeline is the edge of the habitat at which trees can grow. It is too cold for trees and some other plants to grow above the treeline. Climate change is raising temperatures and the snowline is receding, or moving higher up the mountain. This means snow leopards are also having to move higher up the mountains, where there is less food for them to prey on.

A camouflaged snow leopard (circled) searches for food. At higher elevations, there is less vegetation. This means there are fewer grazing animals for the leopards to eat.

Who Got Involved?

Conservationists have always been interested in snow leopards. Modern efforts to protect them first began in the 1970s, when a few organizations were created to pay for research and conservation. Dr. Rodney Jackson began studying snow leopards in Nepal and India in the 1970s. In 2000, he founded the Snow Leopard Conservancy. Dr. George Schaller, who took the first photographs of the snow leopard in the wild, helped to found Panthera in 2006, a global organization devoted to protecting all big cats.

In 2013, the 12 countries where snow leopards roamed finally came together to form the Global Snow Leopard & Ecosystem Protection Program (GSLEP). The GSLEP allowed the agencies of these governments to work with conservation groups such as Panthera, the Snow Leopard Conservancy, the Snow Leopard Trust, and the World Wildlife Fund (WWF).

Dr. George Schaller founded Panthera in 2006. He had been studying big cats and other endangered mammals since the 1950s. Panthera was set up to protect and conserve the world's 36 species of wild cats.

COMMUNITY CONSERVATION

Some communities take their own approach to conservation. The Wakhi people live in the mountains of Afghanistan and Pakistan. In the Wakhi village of Shimshal in Pakistan, the people created their own "nature trust" to manage their community pastureland, educate their community about conservation and environmental issues, and support economic development without damaging their natural resources. The herders of Shimshal combine their traditional ideas of the natural world with modern environmental conservation.

COLLABORATING FOR A CAUSE

Helen Freeman was working as a volunteer at the Woodland Park Zoo in Seattle, Washington, when she first saw a snow leopard. The zoo welcomed two snow leopards from Russia in 1972. Helen was so inspired by her work at the zoo that she went back to university to study animal behavior. In 1981, she founded the Snow Leopard Trust, helping to raise awareness about the species and advising zoos how to care for their snow leopards and improve **captive breeding** programs. She became an expert on the behavior of captive snow leopards. The Snow Leopard Trust broadened its horizons and began to work on conservation in the wild. It was the first organization to protect the snow leopard by helping the human populations that share their habitat.

Raising Global Awareness

For decades, relatively small organizations had been working within local communities in different countries. When GSLEP signed the Bishkek Declaration in 2013, snow leopard conservation became **transnational**. The 12 snow leopard range countries that signed the declaration agreed to make the snow leopard and protection of the ecosystem a priority. Their seven-year goal was to create 20 protected areas of snow leopard habitat by the year 2020. The program was designed to support snow leopard conservation and the high mountain communities.

GSLEP meets every year at conferences and committee meetings. It partners with conservation groups and researchers worldwide. Its goals include raising global awareness, collecting scientific data, preventing poaching, working with local communities on conservation programs, and keeping safe "corridors" for snow leopards across international boundaries.

In 2007, Dr. B. Munkhtsog, a Mongolian scientist, asked Dr. Rodney Jackson (left) for help. In spring that year, **camera traps** and **radio collars** were used to track and count snow leopard populations in Mongolia.

SNOW LEOPARD DAYS

International Snow Leopard Day is celebrated on October 23 each year. This is the day that the 12 snow leopard countries signed the Bishkek Declaration. At that meeting, the countries also declared 2015 to be the Year of the Snow Leopard. Zoos, conservation groups, and governments focused on the snow leopard and the threats it faces.

ENDANGERED OR VULNERABLE?

In 2016, based on the findings of their research, the IUCN and experts like Dr. Rodney Jackson decided that the snow leopard should be relisted as Vulnerable, instead of Endangered, on the Red List. More accurate estimates of numbers seemed to indicate that it was no longer as rare as was once believed. However, not all conservationists and scientists agreed with the IUCN. GSLEP argued against the reclassification until researchers and communities could confirm more accurate counting of numbers. They argued that scientists had only studied about 2 percent of the snow leopard's habitat. Many experts worry that changing its status from Endangered to Vulnerable will make it harder to raise money and introduce laws to protect snow leopards.

Observing the Snow Leopards

Experts try to make an estimate of the number of snow leopards in the wild by looking for tracks and other physical evidence. The most important tool for observing and counting the snow leopard is a camera trap, which is a camera activated by a motion detector. The camera is set up in the wild where animals are thought to roam. Any movement triggers the camera to start recording a video.

Setting camera traps is a difficult task. Snow Leopards live in remote, snowy mountains. Researchers have to climb, walk, or ski for hundreds of miles to place traps across a wide area. In some countries, conservation organizations employ and train local hunters or forestry workers to place and monitor the camera traps.

Forestry workers set up a camera trap in Russia. It has a motion detector and is attached to the tree with straps.

COLLABORATING FOR A CAUSE

Dr. Rodney Jackson was the first researcher to use radio collars to track snow leopards. From 1981 to 1985, Jackson and his team followed the movements of five snow leopards in Nepal, tracking them from the radio signals given off by their collars. Jackson founded the Snow Leopard Conservancy to focus on community-based **stewardship** of the snow leopard. Today, radio collars, camera traps, and genetic research are all methods used to track and protect the snow leopard populations in the wild.

A snow leopard wearing a radio collar photographed in the Himalayas in India.

SNOW LEOPARD GRID

In 2017, the WWF and New York University tested a new method for counting and monitoring the movements of snow leopards in Russia's Altai Mountains. Named the Snow Leopard Grid, this method collects data, or information, from camera traps, as well as field observations, and uses a computer model to analyze the data. The data also includes reports about the number of snow leopards sold illegally by poachers.

Community Planning

The snow leopard plays an important part in the folklore of many people living in Central Asia's high mountains. It is respected by the people. But today, these communities often survive on less than $2 a day, and the snow leopard is a threat. Teaching local people about modern environmental conservation plays an important part in protecting the snow leopards. More important, however, is providing real solutions for the problem of hunting by herders and poachers. Conservation programs have been developed to prevent poaching by paying families for every animal they lose to snow leopards. This keeps herders from attacking the big cats. Paying hunters to help count and monitor snow leopards also stops them from poaching.

The WWF helps communities to improve fencing and pens where they keep their sheep and goats. This makes it harder for snow leopards to prey on their animals.

COLLABORATING FOR A CAUSE

Snow Leopard Enterprises was created in 1998 by the Snow Leopard Trust. It aimed to fight the human poverty that lay behind the snow leopards' conflict with people. Snow Leopard Enterprises buys handicrafts made by the women in Mongolian herder communities, and resells them to customers around the world online and in stores. This increases a herding family's income. To participate in this program, all members of the community have to agree to protect the snow leopard and its wild prey from poachers. The community receives a cash bonus each year, which they lose if any poaching takes place. The program encourages communities to work together and with conservation programs, and also improves the quality of their lives.

The Snow Leopard Conservancy established Savings and Credit Associations in four communities in Nepal. Villagers put a small sum in a savings fund every month. Loans and interest from the fund are spent on the community and on projects that contribute to snow leopard conservation.

Increasing Numbers

The GSLEP had set an ambitious goal with their seven-year "20 by 2020" plan. In the first year, the participating countries had created 23 areas of protected habitat for the snow leopards. Programs such as the Snow Leopard Grid counting and monitoring program have since reported an increase in the number of snow leopards. In 2018, the Snow Leopard Grid program counted 38 adult leopards and 23 cubs in Russia's Altai Mountains. This was an increase in numbers from 2017. Snow leopards in the area are breeding. The researchers also found a female with four newborn cubs. It seems that snow leopard numbers are recovering, but the species is still not out of danger.

Snow leopards live alone and only meet to mate. Female leopards usually give birth to two or three cubs about 100 days after mating. The cubs will stay with the mother for 18 to 22 months.

CAPTIVE BREEDING PROGRAMS

Zoos play an important role in species conservation. Animals in zoos raise awareness among people who might never see animals in the wild. In 1986, the first snow leopard arrived in a North American zoo. Since then, many snow leopards have been born in captivity. Captive breeding helps scientists to study biology, genetics, and behavior. North America's Snow Leopard Species Survival Plan (SSP) works with zoos to match adult snow leopards for mating. Today, 68 North American zoos have snow leopards.

COLLABORATING FOR A CAUSE

In 2014, the World Wildlife Fund (WWF) started a project with six poachers in the Altai Mountains of Russia. The men were encouraged to help monitor camera traps in the area. They were paid for every photograph of a snow leopard. The snow leopard population began to increase. This encouraged the WWF to expand the project into other areas, such as Kyrgyzstan and Tajikistan.

Community Success

Communities that take part in Snow Leopard Enterprises have been able to increase their incomes by up to 40 percent. In 2015, the Kyrgyz village of Enilchek lost their conservation bonus when a snow leopard was poached in their area. The poachers were caught on camera! When the community discovered that a man from their village had helped the poachers, they met with his family. The family agreed to pay the families who had lost their annual bonus. The bonus is about $86 per family, a large amount for families who earn less than $400 a year. More camera traps were put in the area.

Camera traps and local people can help to catch poachers. The community helps government anti-poaching teams in Kyrgyzstan to rescue animals that have been poached.

COLLABORATING FOR A CAUSE

Successful local community programs have helped to increase the number of snow leopards in the wild:

- In Mongolia, more than 400 families participate in the Snow Leopard Enterprises handicraft program
- In Western Tuva, Russia, 70 herders were taught how to protect **livestock**. Since then, none of their herds have been attacked, and the number of snow leopards in the area has increased.
- In Gilgit-Baltistan, Pakistan, a community livestock insurance plan funded by villagers and a conservation grant compensates for any livestock killed by snow leopards
- In the Indian **Himalayas**, tourism has increased community income and changed attitudes. Sightings of snow leopards have increased from 1 to 3 each year to several each week.

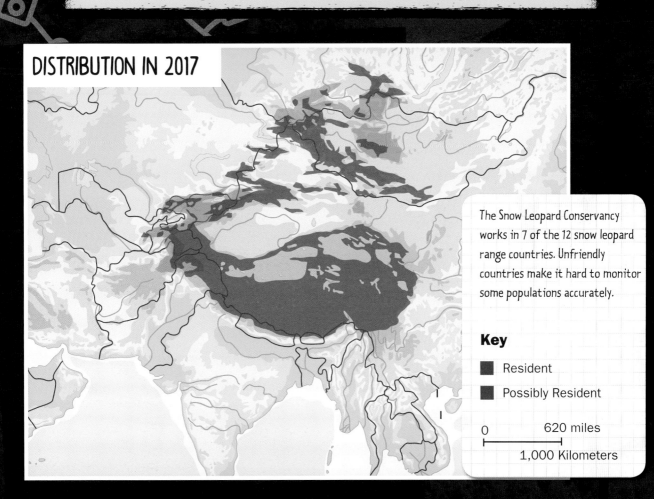

DISTRIBUTION IN 2017

The Snow Leopard Conservancy works in 7 of the 12 snow leopard range countries. Unfriendly countries make it hard to monitor some populations accurately.

Key

■ Resident

■ Possibly Resident

0   620 miles

1,000 Kilometers

What Does the Future Hold?

Some snow leopard conservationists were worried when the IUCN changed the snow leopard's status from Endangered to Vulnerable. However, the global network of conservation groups, local communities, and government agencies have not slowed down their efforts to save the snow leopard and its habitat. There remain two goals for the future: to continue to observe and monitor the number of snow leopards living in the wild; and to stop illegal poaching.

An anti-poaching team in the Altai Mountains in Russia is trained in how to remove snares from animals. Snares have now been cleared from two valleys where snow leopards live in Argut. One of the team members is a former snow leopard poacher.

COLLABORATING FOR A CAUSE

No one is sure how many snow leopards live in the mountains of Central and South Asia. To help solve this problem, the GSLEP has launched the Population Assessment of the World's Snow Leopards (PAWS) plan. Scientists use sampling, which means counting the number of cats in one small area, or sample area. The PAWS program will use camera traps, field observation, and other scientific methods to count snow leopards and then use **statistical analysis** to create accurate estimates. Local conservation groups will use the same methods. Several workshops have been held to train local workers in these methods.

Shannon Kachel, a snow leopard scientist, in the mountains of eastern Kyrgyzstan. She is using electrical signal receiving equipment to locate a female snow leopard that is wearing a radio collar.

FIGHTING WILDLIFE CRIME

In 2016, a report on wildlife crime estimated that 220 to 450 snow leopards are killed every year. At least half of the animals are traded illegally. Experts know that the trade in pelts and body parts is run by **organized crime**. Only a few snow leopards are killed on purpose by poachers, but criminals pay herders and hunters for the snow leopards they have killed to protect livestock, or in the traps they set for other animals. This makes it tempting for local people to kill snow leopards. The International Consortium on Combating Wildlife Crime was founded in 2010 by five international organizations, including INTERPOL and the Convention on International Trade in Endangered Species. Working together, these organizations hope to improve wildlife crime databases and law enforcement across the 12 snow leopard countries.

Saving Other Species

As a keystone species, the snow leopard plays an important role in the mountains of Central and South Asia. The lessons learned from snow leopard conservation are useful in conservation efforts to save other threatened species around the world. Panthera is an organization that focuses on the conservation of the world's big cats. They have programs to help fight the threats against cheetahs, jaguars, leopards, lions, pumas, snow leopards, and tigers.

They are fighting to end poaching, prevent conflict between humans and big cats, and protect the habitat of wild cats. Like the snow leopard, many big cats are keystone species. Their survival helps to ensure healthy ecosystems that support all life, including the lives of people.

Jaguars live in Central and South America. They are threatened by loss of habitat due to human settlement expansion, as well as by farmers and poachers. The IUCN Red List classifies them as Near Threatened (NT).

SIBERIAN IBEX

The Siberian ibex is an important prey for snow leopards. The ibex is a type of mountain goat that is under threat from hunters and poachers. The decline in ibex numbers is one reason for snow leopards preying on livestock, which in turn puts them under threat from people. The predator-prey relationship between the snow leopard and the ibex is important to the fragile ecosystem of high mountains. The IUCN Red List currently classifies Siberian ibex as being of Least Concern.

KEYSTONE CATS

Most species of wild cats are at risk. Tigers, close cousins of the snow leopard, are perhaps the most endangered. Some subspecies of tigers have less than 100 individual animals living in the wild. Big cats around the world face the same threats. Their habitat and food supply are shrinking from human development and climate change. But the biggest threat to big cats is illegal hunting. The IUCN Red List currently classifies tigers as Endangered.

What Can You Do to Help?

The snow leopard is back from the brink of extinction, but it is far from safe. Saving snow leopards takes commitment from everyone. The mountains of Asia are far away, but there are still some small things you can do to help. Like all species, the snow leopard is facing a threat from climate change. Actions in North America affect the climate in Asia.

One of the best ways to save energy is to turn the thermostat down. If you turn the thermostat down by 7 to 10 degrees from its normal setting for 8 hours per day, the energy saving will be up to 10 percent. Perhaps you could send the money your family saves to Snow Leopard Enterprises instead!

Conservationists and researchers can't fight climate change on their own. We can all be part of a global effort to stop climate change and reverse the effects of **global warming**. Personal choices such as reducing waste and saving energy will make a difference to the world if we all try to make an effort.

You can learn more about the work of conservationists at organizations such as the Snow Leopard Trust. Follow the #snowleopard and #paws hashtags on social media and help to spread the word.

SPREAD THE WORD

You may not be able to travel to see the snow leopards, but you can learn more about them. Spreading information and educating people is a great way to help. Here are some ideas you can try:

- International Snow Leopard Day is held on October 23 every year. Why not get your class involved? Prepare a short talk and presentation on the work of the conservation groups working with snow leopards. Make some posters to advertise your talk, and list the websites of the groups you are going to talk about.

- Organize a car wash, bake sale, or plush toy sale and donate the money to one of the snow leopard organizations.

- Write your elected representative or local newspaper and ask them to support the international groups working for climate change.

Learning More

Books

Anderson, Justin, and Patrick Benson. *Snow Leopard: Ghost of the Mountain*. Candlewick Press, 2019.

Gish, Melissa. *Snow Leopards* (Living Wild). Creative Paperbacks, 2017.

Hinman, Bonnie. *Keystone Species that Live in the Mountains*. Mitchell Lane Publishing, 2015.

Miceler, Jon. *Seeking the Snow Leopard.* Tumblehome Learning, Inc., 2017.

On the Web

www.snowleopard.org/
The website of the Snow Leopard Trust, with information about the snow leopard and the trust's programs across Central Asia, including Snow Leopard Enterprises.

www.panthera.org/cat/snow-leopard/
The website of Panthera, with information about the snow leopard and other endangered big cats, such as the tiger, the puma, and the leopard.

snowleopardconservancy.org/
The website of the Snow Leopard Conservancy, with information about the snow leopard and the trust's programs across south Central Asia.

www.nationalgeographic.com/animals/mammals/s/snow-leopard/
The National Geographic Society's information page about the snow leopard, with videos.

For videos, activities, and more, enter the access code at the Crabtree Plus website below.

www.crabtreeplus.com/animals-back-brink

Access code: abb37

Glossary

apex predators A predator at the top of the food chain with no natural enemies

camera trap A camera that is activated by a motion detector or light sensor

captive breeding Keeping animals in a research center or zoo and finding them a mate

ecosystem All living things in a particular area and how they interact

elevation The height of the land above sea level

extinct Having no living members left

global warming The gradual increase of the average temperature on Earth

habitat The natural surroundings in which an animal or plant lives

Himalayas A mountain range in Central Asia with many of the world's highest peaks, such as Mount Everest

keystone species A species that is so important to other species that if it is removed the ecosystem will change

livestock Farm animals used to generate income through meat or products such as milk, eggs, or wool

motion detector A device that responds to movement, often used to turn on lights or take a photo

natural resources Materials from nature that are useful

organized crime Criminal activity that is planned and controlled by a large, powerful group

outcrops A formation of rocks coming out of the ground

pelts Animal skins that still have the fur or hair on them

predator An animal that kills and eats other animals

prey Animals hunted and killed by another animal for food

radio collars A collar put on a wild animal that sends a radio signal, allowing researchers to track the animal's movements

range The geographic boundary for where a species lives

species A group of similar animals or plants that can breed with one another

statistical analysis Detailed examination of data to understand trends and patterns

stewardship The job of taking care of something, such as the environment

transnational Involving several nations

Tibetan Plateau A large area of raised land in Tibet

Index and About the Author

ABOUT THE AUTHOR
Rachel Stuckey is a writer and editor with 15 years of experience in educational publishing. She has written more than 25 books for young readers on topics ranging from science to sports, and works with subject matter experts to develop educational resources in the sciences and humanities. Rachel travels for half the year, working on projects while exploring the world and learning about our global community.